**To Tatum
for bringing the monsters back to life**

**And a special thanks to: Joan and Kristen for superb
editing and design, Kelley for prepping each canvas,
and Jason for everything else!**

First edition 2010

Library of Congress Cataloging-in-Publication Data is available.

Library of Congress Catalog Card Number 2009026033

ISBN 978-0-7636-3243-4

09 10 11 12 13 14 SCP.10 9 8 7 6 5 4 3 2 1

Printed in Humen, Dongguan, China

This book was typeset in Symbol.
The illustrations were done in acrylic.

Candlewick Press
99 Dover Street
Somerville, Massachusetts 02144

visit us at www.candlewick.com

The Patterson Puppies

and the
Midnight Monster Party

LESLIE PATRICELLI

CANDLEWICK PRESS

It was the middle of the night.
As usual, Petra woke up.
She was afraid of the dark.
She was afraid of the noises.
And she was afraid—
very afraid—of

the Monster.

Andy, Penelope, and Zack

always slept all night long.

But not **Petra**.

"I heard it scratching on the roof," she told Papa.

"I could see its shadow,"
she told Mama.

"You'll be just fine, sweetheart,"
Papa assured her,
and he carried her back to bed.

But Petra wasn't fine.
She was still scared.

Andy, Penelope, and Zack tried to help.

Monsters are scared of my T. rex!

One wave of my magic wand and -POOF- they're gone!

I'll get them with my SUPER-STRENGTH!

But nothing worked for Petra:
not a T. rex, not a wand, not a superhero cape . . .

not even sixteen of her favorite stuffed animals.

The next day Petra was tired.
"I do *not* like the monster," she said.

"Why?" asked Penelope.

"Because," said Petra,
"I know it wants to eat us all up."

"We could give it something else to eat," said Andy.
"Like cookies! Monsters love cookies!
I read it in a book."

"Let's bake some for the monster!" said Penelope.

Petra wasn't sure. But she did love cookies,
so she agreed to try.

Mama helped them bake.
They filled a big plate for the monster—
and ate the rest, of course.

Next they wrote a note.

DEAR MON2TER,
WE HOPE YOU
LIKE THE
COOKIES.
PETRA
ZACK
♡PENELOPE
ANDY

Then they set the table. Everything was just right.

Almost.

When it was bedtime, the puppies were so excited
that none of them could sleep.

Then Papa had a quiet contest.
No one wanted to lose. And finally they nodded off.

During the night, Petra opened her eyes.
She listened. She thought she could hear noises.
She was afraid, so she woke up the others.

"I hear the monster," she whispered.

"I want to see it!" said Andy, hopping out of bed.
"Let's go!"

Petra didn't want to go,
but she didn't want to be left alone either.

They snuck out of their room and down the hall
to the living room . . .

but no one was there.

And no one had eaten the cookies!
So they decided to have a snack.

Then Petra heard something.
She turned around, and there it was . . .

the Monster!

"Quick! Cover your eyes
so it can't see us!" said Zack.
They all covered their eyes.

Petra peeked.
She could not believe
what she saw.

"The monster is hiding," she whispered.
"I think it's scared."

"Monsters don't get scared,"
said Penelope. "*I* do!"

Zack shut his eyes tighter. Andy shivered.
"Don't look at it!" said Andy. "It will eat you up!"

"But it doesn't look like it wants to eat us," said Petra.
"It looks sad."

"I think it needs a cookie," said Petra.
"You can come out, Monster."

The monster peeked. It sniffed.
Finally it rose.
It held sixteen stuffed animals—
four in each arm.

"Hey! I love stuffed animals, too!"
Petra said.

"I love cookies!"
said the monster.

"You can have one,"
said Petra.

The monster wasn't sure, but it *did* love cookies.
So it decided to try.

"Yummy!" said the monster.

"It's a party!" said Petra.

They had so much fun,

Mama and Papa!

"The monster did it!" the puppies shouted.

But Mama and Papa didn't see any monster.
All they saw were four little puppies.

"The monster *was* here!" said Petra.
"I wish you could have seen her. She was so nice.
She loved the cookies. She ate all of them!"

"None for me?" asked Papa.

"You little monsters can clean up this mess first thing in the morning," Mama said.

Then she marched the puppies straight back to bed.

And this time,
Petra went right to sleep.